SOUND Out the Digestive System

Dear Reader

I called this book *Sound Out the Digestive System* because many bodily sounds originate in the digestive system. I thought it would be interesting and fun to find out what's happening inside your digestive system when it makes you burp, gurgle, cough or hiccup!

> "FOLLOW THE JOURNEY THAT FOOD TAKES THROUGH THE DIGESTIVE SYSTEM."

In Chapter Six, you can find out how to look after your digestive system by making sure you consume the right amount of fibre every day. Then you can see if you like the high-fibre recipe "Baked Beans and Bacon Toasted Sandwich" in the next chapter.

I hope you enjoy finding out more about how the digestive system works!

Sharon Parsons

My sincere thanks to the following children for being our models for the recipe in this book:

Lizzie Bollas, Melbourne, Australia

Jackson Pinches, Melbourne, Australia

NELSON
CENGAGE Learning™
For learning solutions, visit cengage.com.au

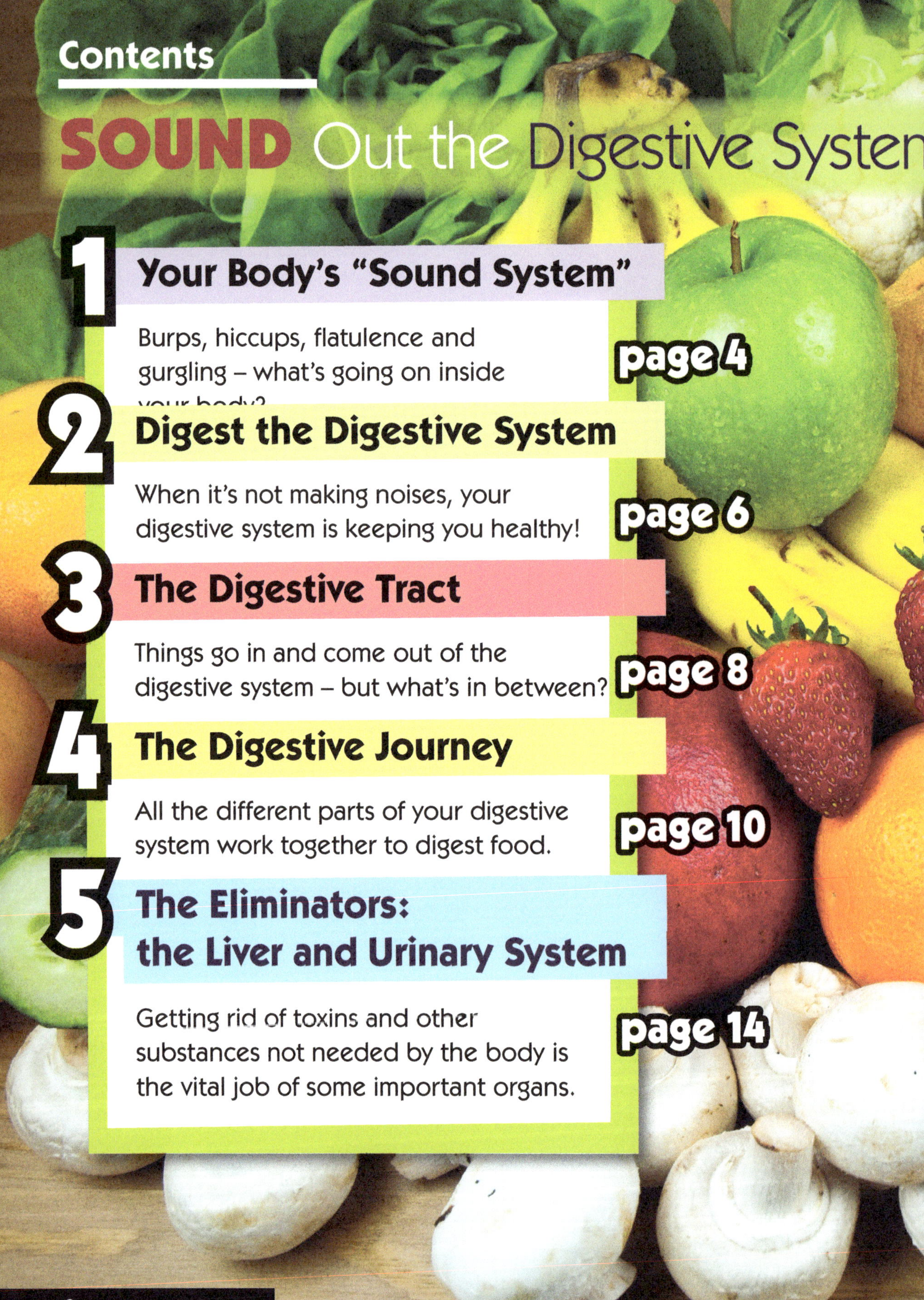

Contents

SOUND Out the Digestive System

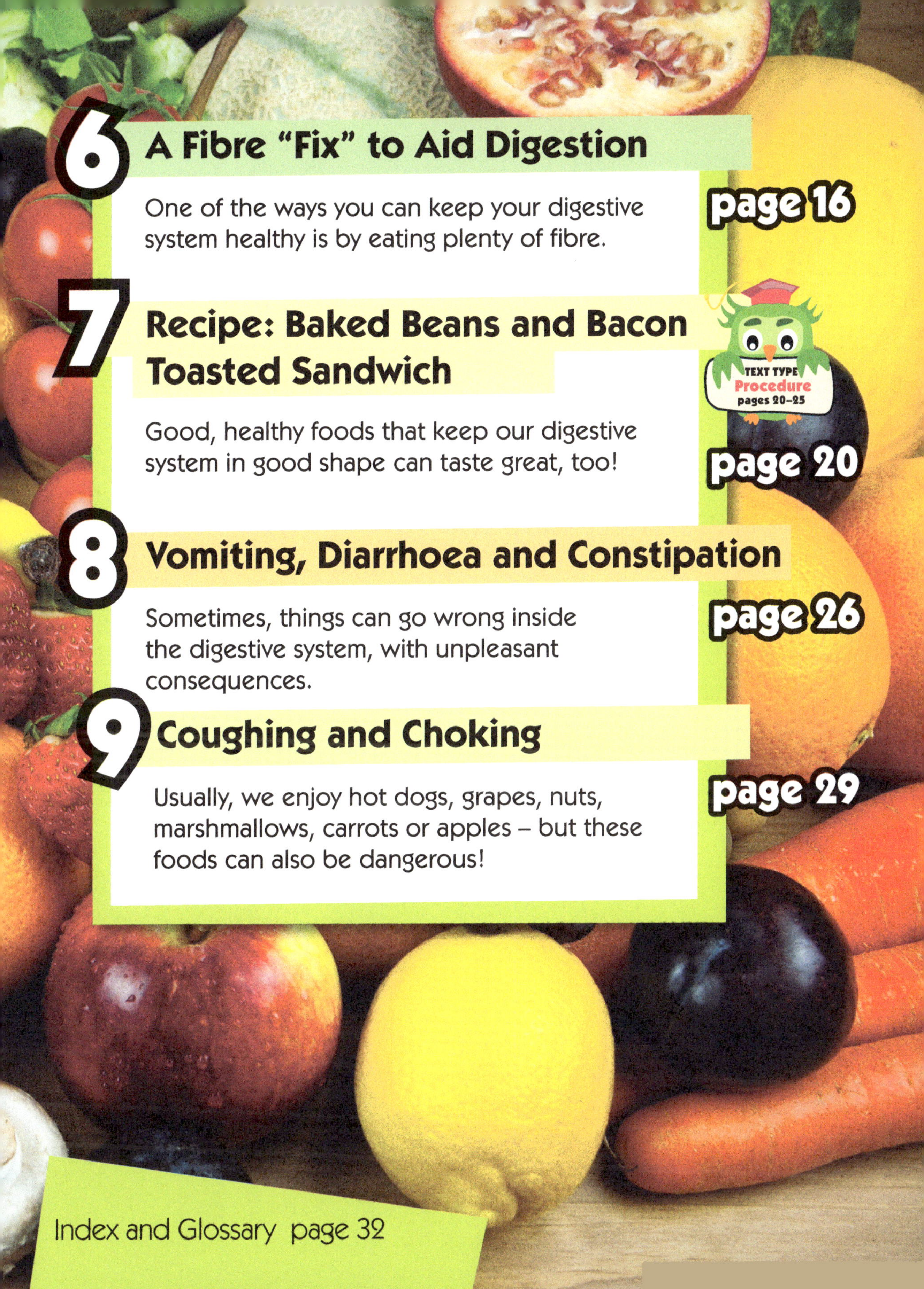

1 Your Body's "Sound System"

Have you ever wondered what's really happening in your body when you burp, hiccup, get flatulence, or when you hear gurgling sounds coming from your abdomen?

The answers can be found in your digestive system, since these sounds are often connected to the breaking down of food and drinks. In order to understand what is causing those sounds it's helpful to understand how your digestive system works after you eat food and drink fluids.

What's borborygmus?

Borborygmus is used to describe bowel sounds (gurgling, rumbling or growling) that are caused by the muscular contractions that move the contents of the stomach along the intestines.

Digestion and Indigestion

The process of digestion is when food is broken down into easy-to-absorb nutrients and particles by the body's digestive system.

Indigestion can happen when people eat too much food too quickly, or if they eat foods that are not right for their bodies. It can make people burp a lot, or feel sick in the stomach and bloated. Some people may also feel like vomiting.

2 Digest the Digestive System

Remember to chew food properly.

yoghurt

The digestive system is an amazing part of the body that works for 24 hours each day to keep the body in good health. People can help their digestive systems to work well by:

- making healthier food and drink choices
- chewing food properly
- feeling relaxed when eating.

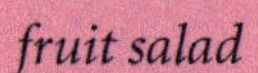

fruit salad

baked beans

eggs

It helps to be relaxed when you eat.

fresh milk

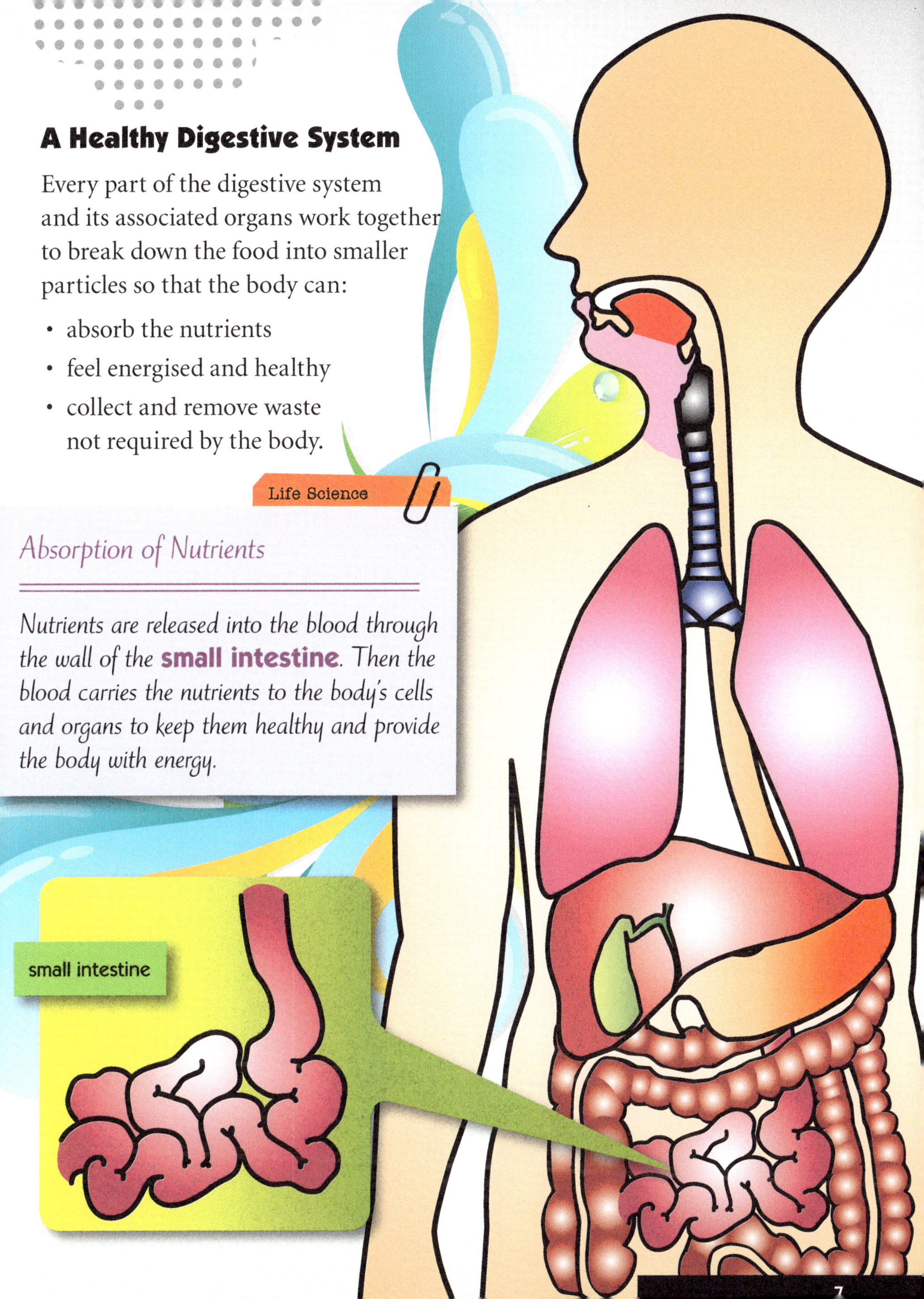

A Healthy Digestive System

Every part of the digestive system and its associated organs work together to break down the food into smaller particles so that the body can:

- absorb the nutrients
- feel energised and healthy
- collect and remove waste not required by the body.

Life Science

Absorption of Nutrients

Nutrients are released into the blood through the wall of the **small intestine***. Then the blood carries the nutrients to the body's cells and organs to keep them healthy and provide the body with energy.*

3 The Digestive Tract

The most important part of the digestive system is a series of muscle-lined tubes and organs called the digestive tract. Food passes through each part of the digestive tract in turn, from the mouth to the anus.

MEDICAL NAMES

Medical professionals also refer to the digestive tract as the "alimentary canal" or the "gastrointestinal tract".

Length of the Tract

The digestive tract is about nine to ten metres long in adults and about seven metres long in children.

Depending on the person and the kind of food eaten, it can take between 12 and 24 hours for food to pass through the digestive tract.

In less healthy people it can take 48 hours or more – longer periods may mean that the person is constipated.

A healthy meal improves food digestion.

Gurgling Sounds in the Digestive Tract

Gurgling sounds during digestion are normal. They come from either the **stomach** or the small intestine as food is digested and moves along the digestive tract. The muscles in the small intestine move partly digested food, air, water, gas, fibre and other substances. The muscles cause a swirling motion which can cause gurgling sounds. The medical term for this process is peristalsis.

If your stomach is empty the gurgling sounds may be louder until you eat some food. If the gurgling is excessive, the body may be sending "warning signals" about a more serious health problem.

GRRR!

"My tummy is making loud gurgling sounds today!"

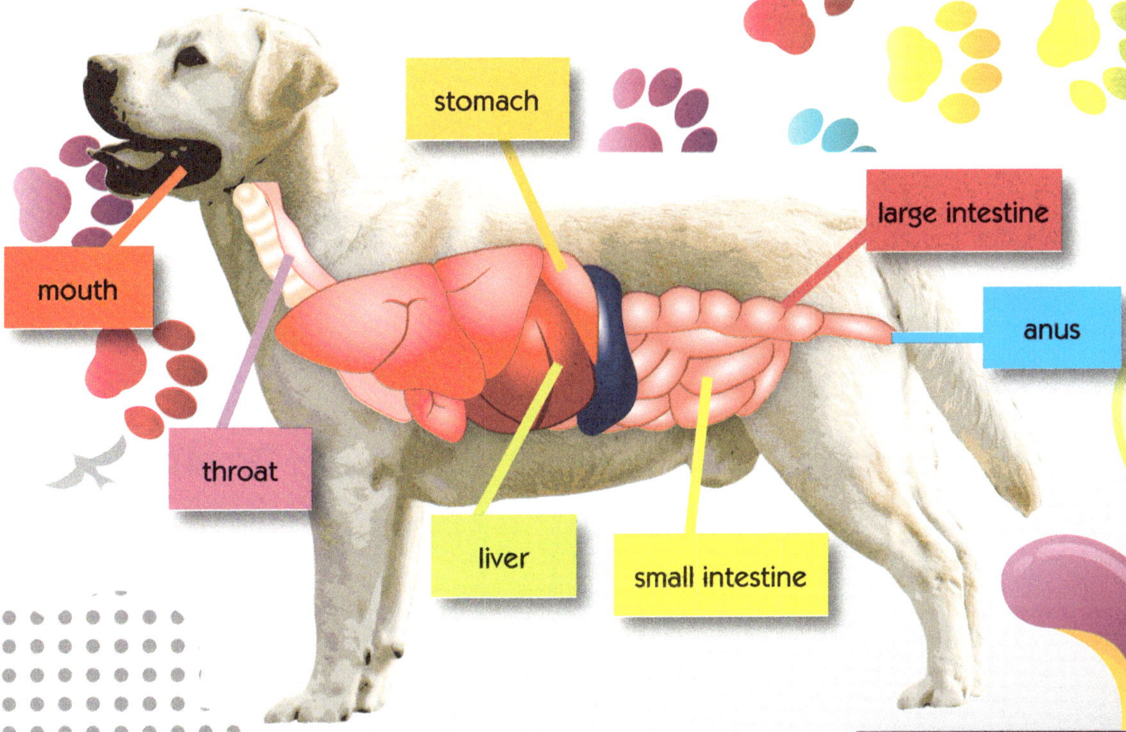

stomach

large intestine

mouth

anus

throat

liver

small intestine

4 The Digestive Journey

Try not to eat more than a fist-sized amount of food at each meal.

Your digestive system never stops working because food and drinks take many hours to pass through the long digestive tract. Follow the journey that food takes through the digestive system.

1. Mouth

Digestion begins in the mouth because **saliva** has enzymes that help to break down food. People can aid the process of digestion by chewing their food slowly and several times to allow the saliva's enzymes to blend with the food. This also makes it easier to swallow the food.

SALIVA

Saliva is made by the salivary glands in and around the mouth and throat. The glands empty into the mouth through ducts. Saliva not only helps to digest food but also cleans the mouth and kills germs.

pharynx

2. Pharynx

Air and food pass through the **pharynx** in the throat.

3. Oesophagus

The digestive journey continues with the **oesophagus** on page 12.

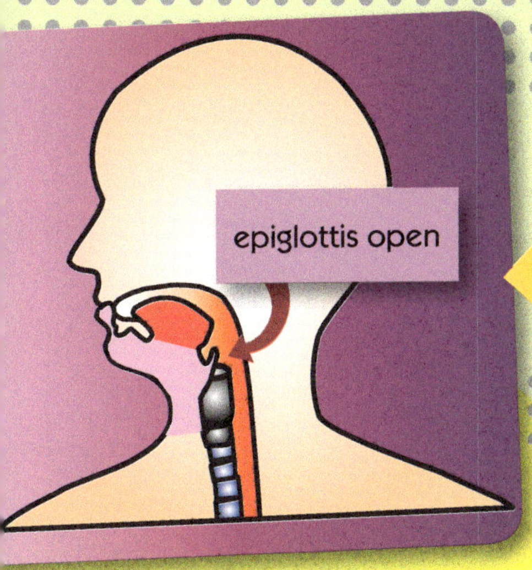

EPIGLOTTIS

The **epiglottis** is a small flap of tissue in the throat that prevents food or drink from getting into the **trachea** when a person swallows.

It's like a trapdoor to the trachea.

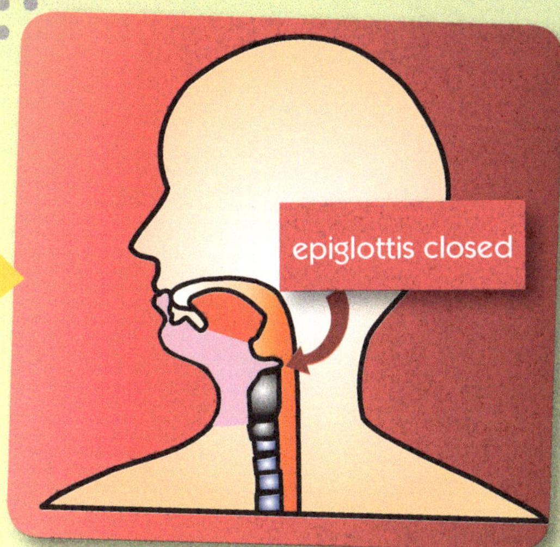

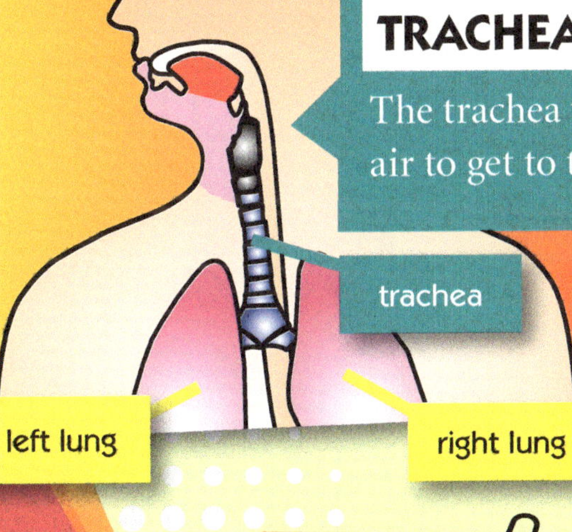

TRACHEA

The trachea tube allows air to get to the lungs.

"I've got the hiccups ... again!"

Hiccups in the Epiglottis

A hiccup is a spasm in your diaphragm that makes you suck in air, which is stopped by your epiglottis quickly closing. The "hic" is the sound of your epiglottis shutting off the airflow. Scientists don't know what causes hiccups, but some medical professionals believe that they may be caused by certain foods and drinks, or even by indigestion.

Health

What Causes Choking?

When the epiglottis doesn't close quickly enough, a person can choke on food that goes into the trachea. Read more on pages 29–31.

3. Oesophagus

This soft tube of tissue is lined with muscles that move food down from the **pharynx** to the **stomach**.

4. Stomach

The pouch-shaped **stomach** is about the size of a person's fist and it is where natural acids further digest the food.

5. Small Intestine

The **small intestine** is called "small" because its diameter is not as wide as that of the **large intestine** – it is about five to six times longer than the large intestine. The small intestine "sits" in a coil shape in the centre of the large intestine. Partly digested food passes through three sections of the small intestine during the final stages of digestion:

- Duodenum (about 30 centimetres long)
- Jejunum (about one and a half to two and a half metres long)
- Ileum (about five to six metres long).

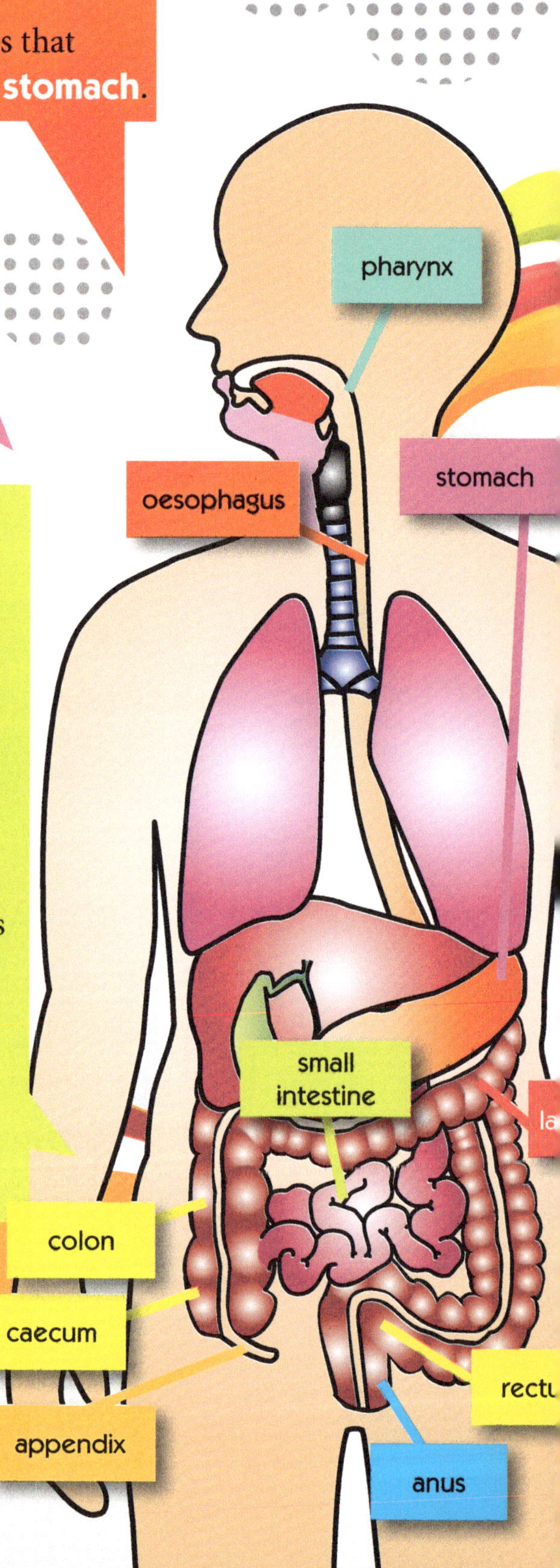

APPENDICITIS

If the **appendix** swells too much, you may feel sharp pains. This condition is called appendicitis.

6. Large Intestine

By the time food reaches the **large intestine**, it has been transformed into a digested liquid. There are many kinds of good bacteria present in the large intestine that aid digestion, produce nutrients and prevent harmful bacteria forming that may cause sickness.

6a. Caecum

The digested liquid passes from the pouch-shaped **caecum** (at the start of the large intestine) into the **colon**.

6b. Colon

This is the longest part of the large intestine. Its total length is about one and a half metres. The main purposes of the **colon** are to:

- form faeces from digested liquid, fibre and water
- regulate the amount of water that passes between the intestine and the body
- use some of the **fibre** to make nutrients for the bacteria in the large intestine to nourish its cells
- move faeces to the **rectum**.

6c. Rectum

This section of the large intestine is about 15 to 20 centimetres long. Faeces are stored in the **rectum** until they leave the body through the **anus**.

7. Anus

The **anus** is the final part of the digestive system.

Health

Burping from the Inside

Burping is normal. Burps come out of your mouth when gas comes up from your stomach. Gas builds up in your stomach when you swallow air along with your food. If you eat or drink too quickly and don't chew your food sufficiently, you can swallow more air, which leads to more burping.

"Burp! Excuse ME!"

5 The Eliminators: the Liver and Urinary System

Liver

The **liver** is the largest organ inside the body. Undigested waste is passed from the small intestine into the liver, which gets rid of any toxins or poisons. Eating healthy foods helps to keep the liver working well.

Largest Organ

The body's largest organ is the **skin**.

Nutrients for the Body

Nutrients are used by the **liver** to make other useful substances, such as bile (in the **gall bladder**) for digestion and glucose for energy.

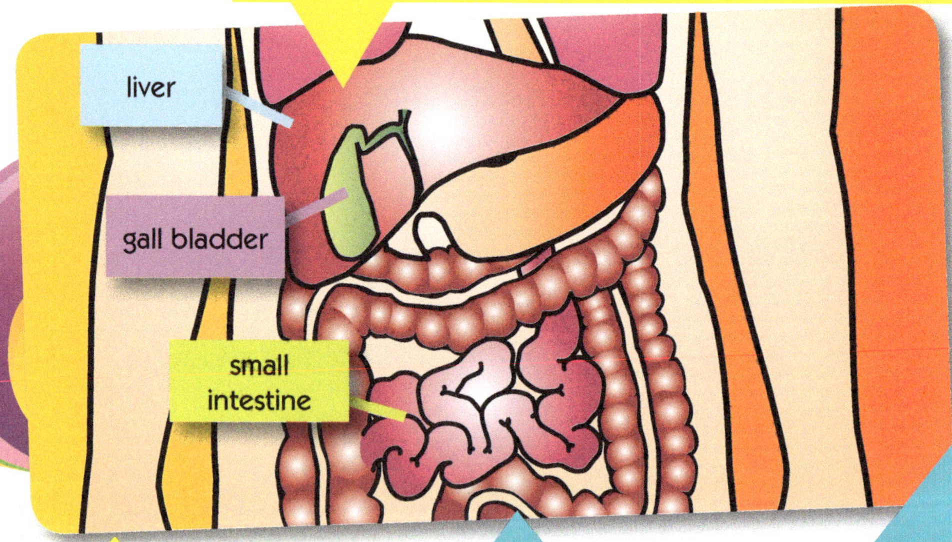

Gall Bladder to Small Intestine

This small pear-shaped organ stores bile until it is needed in the **small intestine**. Bile enables digestion to continue in the small intestine.

Toxins from Liver to Kidneys

The **liver** breaks down the toxins into less toxic or less harmful substances. Then the toxins go to the **kidneys**, the first part of the **urinary system**.

The **Urinary** System

The urinary system works with the digestive system (as well as with the **lungs** and the **skin**) to remove urine and chemicals that the body no longer needs.

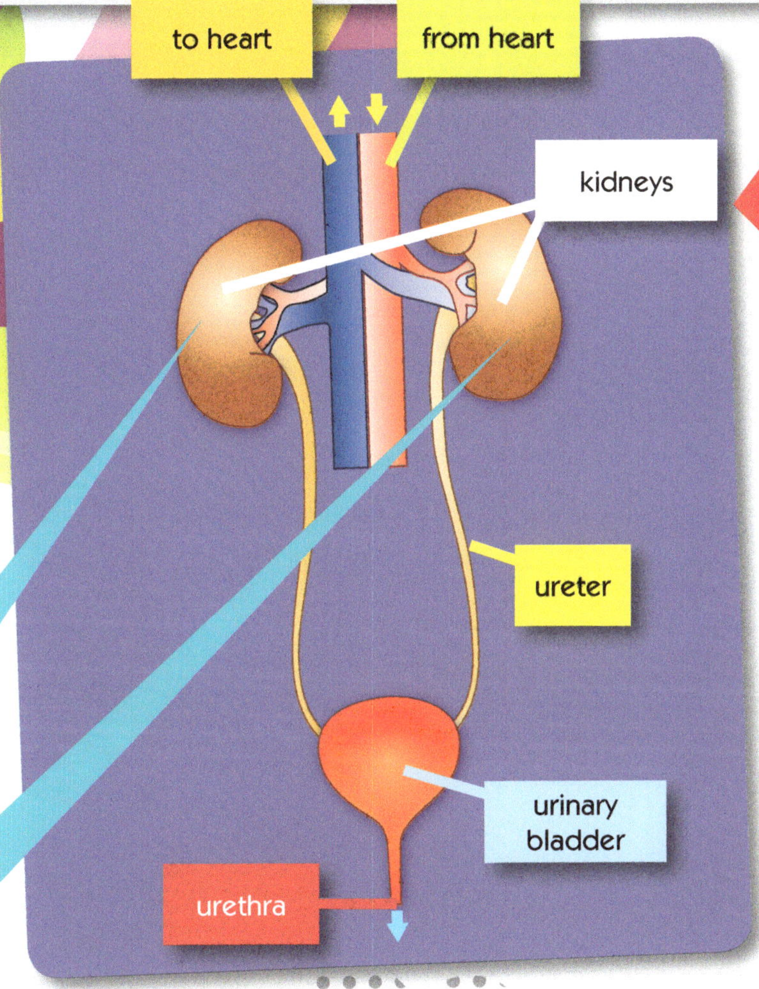

Kidneys and Urea

The **kidneys** also remove urea from the blood. **Urea** is a chemical not needed by the body.

Urine to Bladder to Urethra

In a healthy urinary system, small amounts of urine go to the **urinary bladder** every 10 to 15 seconds. The bladder swells and can hold about two cups of urine for about two to five hours until it leaves the body via the **urethra**.

Urine

Urine travels through the **ureter** tubes between the **kidneys** and the **urinary bladder**, and then out via the **urethra**.

6 A Fibre "Fix" to Aid Digestion

One important way to keep your digestive system healthy is to consume the right amount of dietary fibre every day. Fibre is found in plant-based foods, such as fruit, vegetables, grains, beans and nuts.

Dieticians suggest that primary school children need about 25 to 30 grams of fibre each day to have healthy digestion. Below is a suggested fibre food plan for one day.

Hey kids, this is an example of a healthy fibre plan for one day. The fibre amounts are approximate.

A **Suggested** Fibre **Food** Plan for Kids

Total Fibre for One Day = 31.7 grams

The fibre-rich foods below also contain nutrients in the form of protein, carbohydrates, minerals and vitamins. So start preparing and eating!

Breakfast Total Fibre = 7.6 grams

2 cereal bricks = 3.3 grams fibre

1 banana = 1.9 grams fibre

Orange juice from one orange = 2.4 grams fibre

Muesli or Porridge for Breakfast?

For a change, try half a cup of muesli or porridge for about 3.5 to 4.5 grams of fibre.

2.4 grams fibre

1.9 grams fibre

Add Milk or Yoghurt

Milk and yoghurt have no fibre but they provide other nutrients and they're healthy!

School Snack Total Fibre = 7.3 grams

1 apple (with skin) = 3.3 grams fibre

1 small wholemeal fruit muffin = 4.0 grams fibre

3.3 grams fibre

4.0 grams fibre

School Lunch Total Fibre = 6.8 grams

Fresh strawberries (½ cup) = 2 grams fibre

Wholemeal salad sandwich = 4.8 grams fibre

½ cup = 2 grams fibre

4.8 grams fibre

Wholemeal Bread Fibre

There are about 4.5 grams of fibre in two slices of wholemeal bread.

Where's the Cheese?

Cheese has no fibre but it provides other nutrients and it's healthy!

Nut Allergy

For those with a nut allergy, alternative options include cheese and crackers, or popcorn.

After-School Snack Options

Nuts Total Fibre = 3.5 grams

Mixed nuts (50 grams) = 3.5 grams fibre

Nut Free Total Fibre = 3.5 grams

Crackers (3 medium) = 0.5 grams fibre

Add slices of tomato (4 small) = 1.5 grams fibre

Popcorn (1 cup) = 1.5 grams fibre

2.0 grams fibre

1.5 grams fibre

Dinner Total Fibre = 6.5 grams

Spaghetti bolognaise (1 cup) = 2.5 grams fibre

Cooked vegetables (1 cup) = 4.0 grams fibre

2.5 grams fibre

4.0 grams fibre

Total Fibre in Suggested Food Plan = 31.7 grams

Hey kids: This is a guide only – the exact measurements of your food and drinks are not known.

The amounts of fibre are estimates only.

Talk to your parents if you have food allergies. You can replace some foods with other high-fibre foods. You can also change the order of the foods!

Health

Fibre Rules

Flatulence: Too much fibre can cause flatulence! Find out more on page 19.

Constipation: Not enough fibre can cause constipation. Find out more on page 28.

HEALTH FEATURE

High-Fibre Baked Beans

Baked beans are very high in fibre and nutrients. The toasted sandwich recipe on the next page uses baked beans and it can be made easily at home. But, first ask your parents if you can use an electric frypan or a sandwich maker.

baked beans

Technology

Sandwich Maker Convenience

A sandwich maker is more convenient than a frypan as no butter is required and the sandwich does not need to be flipped.

Beans can cause flatulence in humans.

What Causes Flatulence?

Flatulence is the body's way of removing unwanted or excess gas that has built up in the digestive system. Everyone, every day, experiences flatulence – it's normal.

In public, it's more polite for a person to excuse themselves and go to the toilet or another room when they feel flatulence coming on.

7 Recipe: Baked Beans and Bacon Toasted Sandwich

Goal

To make a baked beans and bacon toasted sandwich.

my baked beans and bacon toasted sandwich

Ingredients

Two slices of wholemeal bread

One slice of cheese

One tomato

Two tablespoons of baked beans

One rasher of bacon with the fat cut off

Two tablespoons of soft butter

ingredients

Equipment

One small paring knife

One butter knife

Two chopping boards

One egg flip

One electric frypan

One plate

equipment

First, wash your hands thoroughly.

Method

Stage 1: Get Organised

Turn on the electric frypan.

Wait until the frypan reaches a low-to-medium heat.

Fry the rasher of bacon for about two minutes each side.

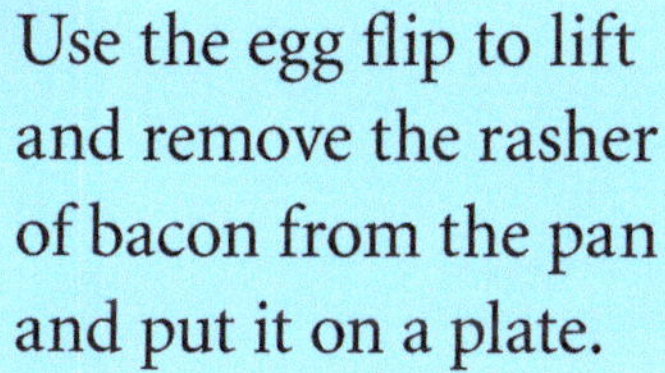

Use the egg flip to lift and remove the rasher of bacon from the pan and put it on a plate.

Method continued on page 22

Method (continued)

Stage 2: Prepare the Toasted Sandwich

Slice the tomato on a chopping board with the paring knife.

Spread the butter on both slices of the wholemeal bread with the butter knife.

Carefully place one slice of bread (butter side down) in the heated electric frypan.

Use the egg flip to gently press the slice of bread down.

Stage 3: Assemble the Toasted Sandwich

Centre the remaining ingredients on the slice of bread in this order.

1. bacon

2. tomato slices

3. baked beans

4. cheese

5. the other slice of bread (butter side up)

Method continued on page 24

Method (continued)

Stage 4: Cook the Toasted Sandwich

Use the egg flip to gently press down on the top of the slice of bread so the bottom slice cooks evenly.

Cook for about three to five minutes in the electric frypan until golden brown.

Use the egg flip to gently lift the sandwich and turn it over so none of the ingredients spill out into the frying pan.

Cook for about three to five minutes in the frypan until golden brown.

Vegetarian Baked Beans Toasted Sandwich

If you are a vegetarian, you could substitute a fried egg for the bacon.

Health

How to Avoid Flatulence!

Chew the baked beans and bacon toasted sandwich well and you shouldn't have flatulence afterwards. And your digestive system will be very pleased, too!

Stage 5: After Cooking the Toasted Sandwich

Turn off the electric frypan.

Use the egg flip to gently lift the toasted sandwich from the frypan onto the plate.

Cut the sandwich in half.

Sit down, relax, eat and enjoy!

After Eating the Toasted Sandwich

Put the dishes in the dishwasher,
or handwash, dry and put away the dishes.

Wipe down the benches.

Wow, the kids cleaned up the kitchen!

Woof ... yes, but there aren't any leftovers. That bacon smelled good!

8 Vomiting, Diarrhoea and Constipation

The body is an efficient organism and will give signals when something isn't healthy on the inside, or will do something to fix it. In the case of constipation, the body is "saying" that there is a problem with digestion. If a person vomits or has diarrhoea it is their body's natural way of getting rid of something unhealthy or even harmful.

bacteria

Vomiting

Vomiting is the process of forcefully expelling digested and undigested food from the stomach through the mouth. It's the body's way of getting rid of harmful substances. Most vomiting, especially where children are concerned, is caused by viruses.

"Me ... owww! I shouldn't have slept here tonight!"

Another common cause of vomiting is food poisoning. Millions of people around the world suffer from food poisoning every year. Two other distressing symptoms of food poisoning are stomach cramps and diarrhoea.

Diarrhoea

Diarrhoea is a disorder that makes you pass very loose, watery stools several times a day. All kinds of factors can cause diarrhoea, including:

- infections from bacteria, viruses and parasites
- food poisoning
- food allergies
- reactions to certain medicines.

"Hurry!"

infection

Diarrhoea and Dehydration

It is common to become dehydrated when you have diarrhoea. Dehydration is occurs when your body loses too much water. Your body also loses electrolytes, which are chemicals that are vital to your body's health. To replace electrolytes, drink fruit juices, water-based soups or sports drinks. A pharmacist may be able to suggest special medication to alleviate the symptoms. Usually, diarrhoea goes away after one or two days but if it continues, it is important to see a doctor.

Constipation

Not enough fibre can cause constipation, which is the body's way of warning that the digestive system has not been able to digest some food properly. Constipation happens when food has not been digested sufficiently for a person to make comfortable bowel movements. There are ways to tell if a person is constipated, including:

- irregular bowel movements
- difficulty passing stools
- hard and dry stools
- a swollen or bloated stomach
- a sore stomach.

"How much longer?"

Daily Bowel Movements

These can vary from person to person and depend on each person's activities and eating habits. On average, people should have about one to two bowel movements each day.

Constipation can be a sign that there are things we should be doing that we are not, for example:

- not eating enough high-fibre foods
- not chewing food well enough
- not drinking enough water
- not doing enough exercise.

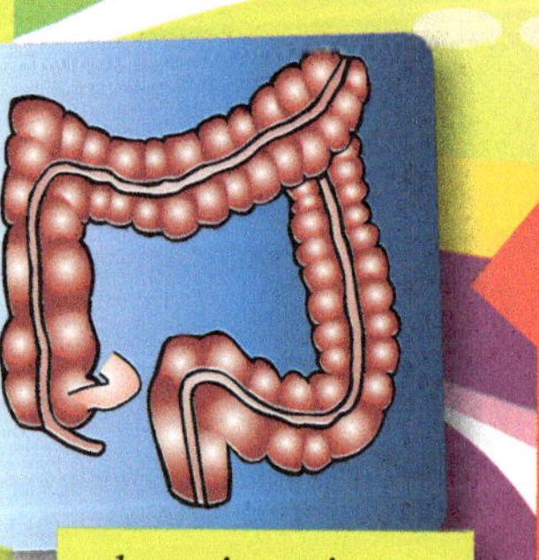

large intestine – also see page 13

Large Bowel

The large bowel is another term for the large intestine. A bowel movement is when faeces or stools pass from the rectum and out of the anus.

9 Coughing and Choking

Coughing can be upsetting but it is the body's natural way of helping to clear food or drink from the trachea or windpipe. But when people choke it is very dangerous.

TRACHEA

The trachea tube allows air to get to the lungs.

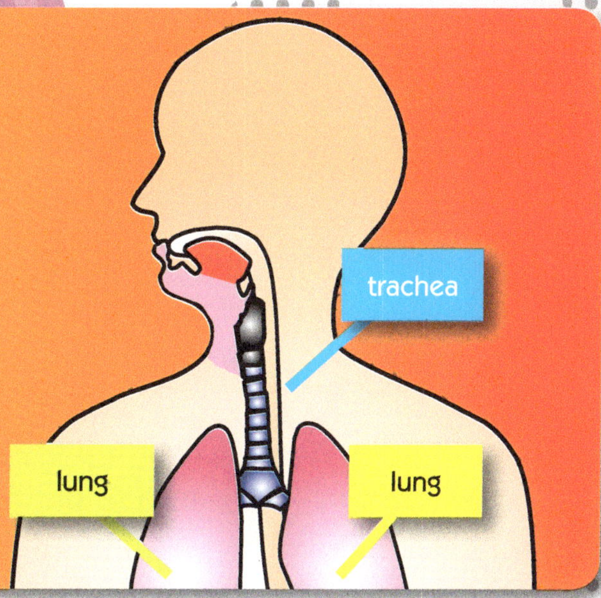

Choking Is Serious

Thousands of people around the world die every year from asphyxiation due to choking. Young children under the age of three have smaller windpipes, so are most at risk. But people of all ages have died from choking on food and other objects.

A Survey on Choking

In the USA, one survey showed that more than 10 000 children under the age of 15 are treated for choking events in hospital emergency departments. Some of the most common items that caused these choking episodes were:

- hot dogs because of their softer, cylindrical shape
- round foods, such as whole grapes, nuts, peanut butter chunks and marshmallows
- large chunks of harder foods, such as carrots and apples.

Why Is Choking so Dangerous?

When someone is severely choking, the food or an object is stopping:

- air from reaching their lungs so within a few minutes they could fall unconscious and die
- oxygen from getting to their brain so they could suffer from brain damage if they survive.

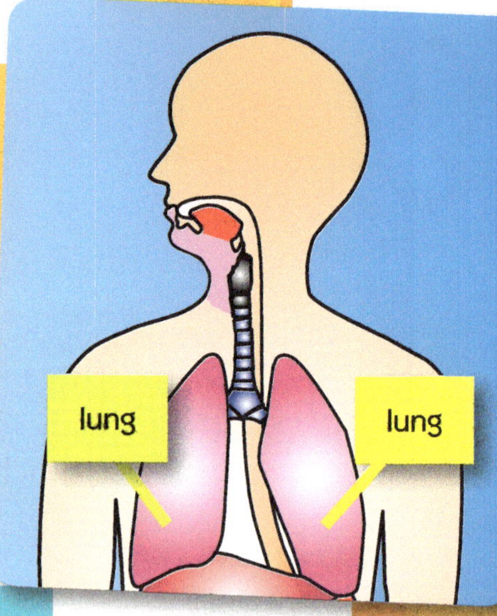

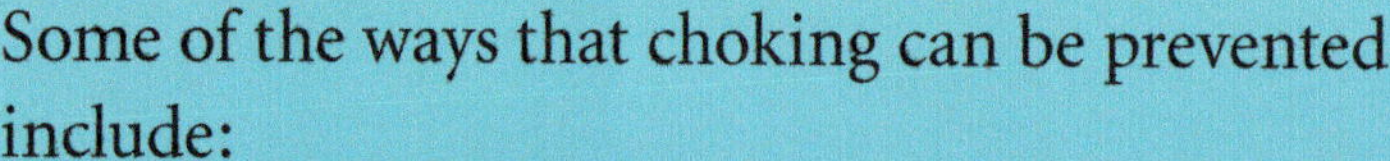

Some of the ways that choking can be prevented include:

- sitting down in a relaxed position when eating
- not talking when the mouth is full
- not gulping down food
- chewing food well before swallowing it
- not putting any objects that are small and solid into the mouth
- not leaving any small and solid items within easy reach of babies and toddlers.

Health

Toys for Youngsters

Toy manufacturers must test their toys before they can sell them. If there are small parts that can easily be broken off and swallowed by a small child, a warning and an older age range should be printed on the packaging. Small solid items cause thousands of young children to choke.

a baby with a safe toy

How to Stop Choking

Most times, a person can cough up the food that is causing them to choke. But in cases of severe choking, what can a bystander do?

Learn one method of first aid for choking, such as the Heimlich manoeuvre.

Dr Heimlich teaches children about first aid for choking cases.

Dr Heimlich

Henry Jay Heimlich (1920–) is a chest surgeon in the USA. When he found out how many people died from choking each year, he worked out a way to help a person suffering a severe choking attack. The Heimlich manoeuvre involves using the air in the lungs to force out the food. Doctor Heimlich's method has saved many lives since he first used it in 1974. The procedure needs to be taught by a health professional.

Health and Safety

Emergency Call Services

Every country has a three-digit emergency number for contacting ambulance, fire or police emergency services. In Australia the number to dial is 000; in New Zealand the number to dial is 111; in the USA and Canada the number to dial is 911; in the European Union the number to dial is 112.

Index

Glossary

asphyxiation The lethal condition of having not enough oxygen in your blood due to being unable to breathe, for example because you are choking

borborygmus The gurgling sounds that can come from the intestines during digestion

dietary fibre A part of some foods that is not digested and absorbed but passes all the way through the digestive tract, helping to keep it healthy

dieticians Medical professionals who specialise in what people should eat

electrolytes Chemicals in the blood that are vital to the body's health, which are lost when the body is dehydrated

faeces Solid waste expelled at the end of the digestion process

nutrients Substances that provide the body with energy and health

peristalsis The way that the muscles of the small intestine contract and loosen to move food along during digestion, which can cause gurgling sounds